What Does My Mom Do in Quarantine?

With my nuclear family in California and my parents in Alabama, Covid-19 separates us indefinitely. This project began as a way for us to stay more connected and resulted in our second children's book. Our perpetual "job" as parents continues to evolve as we try to stay positive and to find the humor in a world that feels upside down. Thank you to my resilient children, my artistic Mom, my editor Dad, and my extraordinary husband, who all wake up with the hope that tomorrow will be even better than today.

Yippidedadumum.

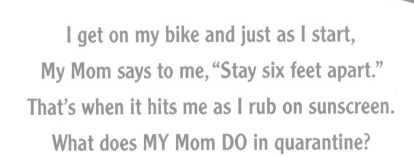

I get on my bike and just as I start,

My Mom says to me, "Stay six feet apart."

That's when it hits me as I rub on sunscreen.

What does MY Mom DO in quarantine?

Joe's Mom designs masks from fabrics so fine
That health workers wear them on the front line.
Could my Mom sew, create that perfect stitch?
She cuts tags in my shirts that make my skin itch.

Pam's Mom makes soap for neighbors we pass.

It smells like gardenia, combined with fresh grass.

Could my Mom clean hands from thumb to pinky?

She makes my cleats shine when they get super stinky.

Jim's Mom hangs paintings in the retirement home.

Sunsets and rainbows for all those alone.

Could my Mom help older people feel fine?

She greets grandma each day with an "I love you" sign.

Sarah's Mom works to discover a cure,
Counting on her to help Covid for sure.
Could my Mom fight an infectious disease?
When I have to get shots, it's her finger I squeeze.

Henry's Mom performs on the Peloton app,
Makes exercise from home feel like a snap.
Could my Mom start classes, help people stay fit?
When running a mile, she won't let me quit.

Greg's Mom develops a tracing profile
That tracks people who leave their house for a while.
Could my Mom design new tech for your phone?
She crashed only twice when flying my drone.

Logan's Mom meditates, breathing so slow.
To live in the present makes her skin glow.
Could my Mom relax and try to sit still?
Her deep breaths are loud when my milk takes a spill.

Austin's Mom bakes her famed cherry tart.

Pastries, fresh bread with yeast as a start.

Could my Mom create sugar treats that are fun?

With slice-and-bake cookies, she burns only one.

Mark's Mom works in a food bank all year,
While the pandemic sustains a global fear.
Could my Mom stock all the things that are key?
She bought one hundred hand gels and mounds of TP.

Daniel's Mom teaches a math class on Zoom.

At times, extra kids end up in her room.

Could my Mom host talks on a computer screen?

My sister says no, but she's a typical teen.

Kathy's Mom anchors for prime time news.

She's vocal about her political views.

Could my Mom report events that we crave?

Most nights, she tells Dad how well we behave.

Payton's Mom builds homes for people in need,

Providing shelter and food and even something to read.

Could my Mom construct? Is that my Mother?

She used planks from our floor to build a ramp
for my brother.

Julia's Mom authors best-selling books.

All fiction novels with realistic hooks.

Could my Mom tell stories with characters too?

She writes poems about jobs that many Moms do.

Su's Mom helps children who need extra care,
Tutors and counsels when life is unfair.
Could my Mom find ways to create opportunity?
She put a quote on our fence calling for unity.

What my Mom does now cannot be debated.
Her job is to make sure that we stay elated!

She's a baker, a seamstress, a scientist and a nurse,

An artist, a teacher, an author of verse,

An instructor, a builder, a reporter you know,

An engineer, a counselor, an athlete and so...

What my Mom does now is not a big mystery.

She's keeping us calm as we live through history.

So one day, I ask her,

"What's the most important part
of quarantine?"

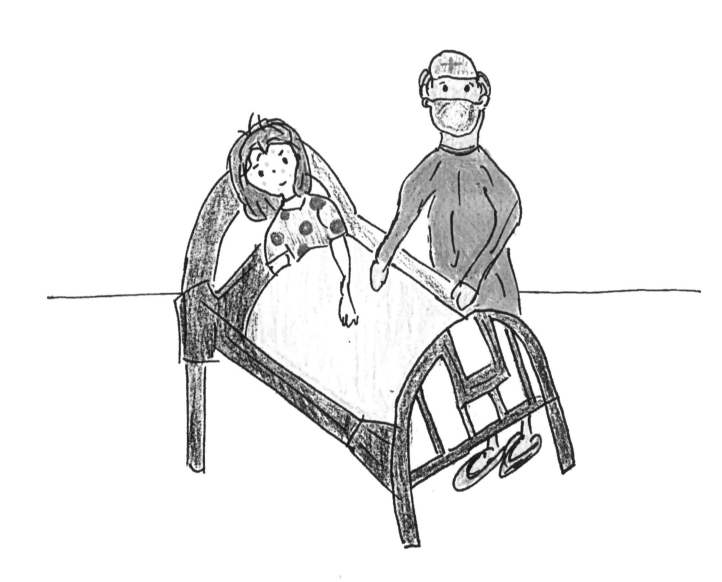

Her reply,
"That the world stays safe until
we find a vaccine."

About the Author

Lisa Ott lives in Burlingame, California, with her husband, Greg, and three children: Sarah, Daniel and Julia. Publishing this book helped her reduce the stress catalyzed by the events of 2020.

About the Illustrator

Pam Koch lives in Mobile, Alabama, with her husband of 51 years, Henry. Her quarantine gift was creating this book with her daughter and grandchildren.

CPSIA information can be obtained
at www.ICGtesting.com
Printed in the USA
BVHW021541191220
595970BV00002B/11